LEVEL 2 READER

Lalaloopsy
Sew Magical! Sew Cute!

Snow Day!

By Jenne Simon
Illustrated by Prescott Hill

SCHOLASTIC INC.

ISBN 978-0-545-58123-3

12 11 10 9 8 7 6 5 4 3 2 1   13 14 15 16 17 18/0

Printed in the U.S.A.   40

Designed by Angela Jun
First printing, September 2013

It was a cold winter day in Lalaloopsy Land.
Mittens Fluff 'N' Stuff and Ivory Ice Crystals
looked outside.
The first snow was falling.

"The snow looks so bright," said Mittens.
Ivory agreed. "It's a winter wonderland!"
"So what are we doing inside?" asked Mittens.
"Let's go!"

First, Ivory wanted to build a snowman.
Once the girls started building, they couldn't stop!

Then Mittens wanted to go sledding.
The hill was faster than she'd thought!
When she and Ivory got to the bottom,
they bumped into an old friend.

"Holly Sleighbells!" cried Mittens. "Come join our snow day!"

"I'd love to," said Holly. "I know just what we should do next. . . ."

"Snowball fight!" cried Holly.
SPLAT! A snowball exploded at Ivory's feet.
"Oh, no you didn't!" she laughed.
Soon snowballs were flying in every direction.

"Enough!" cried Mittens, falling into the snow.
"That gives me another great idea," said Holly.
She lay down and spread her arms.
"Snow angels!" cheered Ivory and Mittens.

When their snow angels were perfect, the girls
stood up and dusted themselves off.
"What should we do now?" asked Holly.
"I know," said Ivory. "Let's check out the pond."

At the pond, they saw something wonderful. Someone was doing a perfect spin on the center of the ice.

It was their friend Swirly Figure Eight!

The girls watched as Swirly skated.
With a quick turn, she began to glide backward.
A moment later, she was flying through the air!

Swirly spotted her friends and skated over.
"Your moves are incredible!" said Holly.
Swirly blushed. "Thanks! Would you girls like to skate with me?"

"Absolutely!" said Mittens.
"I'd love to," said Ivory.
Holly looked nervous. "I . . . I think I'll just watch from here," she said.

"But you'll miss all the fun," cried Mittens.
"You don't have to do fancy spins and jumps to
have a good time on the ice," said Swirly.

The girls stood in line to pick up skates.
"I've never been ice-skating before," Holly
admitted. "I don't know how to skate."
"We'll teach you," said Ivory.

Skates

"Just remember that practice makes perfect," said Swirly. "You can't learn to do something unless you try."

"Okay," said Holly. "I guess I can give ice skating a chance."

Swirly, Ivory, and Mittens glided out onto
the ice.
Holly wobbled.

Holly's friends showed her how to balance.
They showed her how to push off against the ice.
And how to stop.
But Holly just trembled, fumbled, and stumbled.

Holly kept trying.

With every turn around the ice, her skates grew steadier.

Finally, Holly felt ready to ice-skate on her own.

Holly slid toward the center of the ice.
But before she could stop herself, she tumbled
to the ground.

"Ouch!" cried Holly. "I scraped my leg!"

"Holly, are you okay?" asked Mittens.

"Let's get you to the first-aid cart," said Ivory.

"Our friend Rosy will fix you up in a jiffy!" said Swirly.

The girls helped Holly over to their
friend's first-aid cart.
Rosy Bumps 'N' Bruises was waiting with a
bandage and a smile.

Rosy looked at Holly's leg.

"That scrape isn't so bad," said Rosy. "It will get better in no time."

"But my skating won't," said Holly. "I'm terrible!"

"It doesn't matter how many times you fall," said Swirly.

"Only that you get back up," said Rosy.

Holly took a deep breath. "Okay, girls, let's try skating again!"

Mittens, Ivory, Swirly, and Rosy walked
Holly back to the pond.
They helped her get her balance.
They supported her when she felt shaky.

And they held her hands when she felt nervous.

"I have the best friends!" Holly told them. "It's nice to have you to pick me up when I fall!"

The girls went around the pond again and again.

Holly's skates grew steadier.

Soon she felt ready to try skating on her own.

Swirly gave her hand a squeeze.
"You can do it, Holly," Swirly whispered.
"You can ice-skate!"

And as the sun began to set over Lalaloopsy Land, Holly did.

"You did it!" Swirly cried.
Mittens smiled. "I know the perfect way
to celebrate."

Holly looked around the table at all her friends.
"Let's go ice-skating again tomorrow!" she said.
Swirly was surprised. "Are you sure?"
Holly smiled. "Well, practice makes perfect!"